"WHY DID I DO THAT? BECAUSE I WANTED IT. BECAUSE I NEEDED IT."

NINA BERBEROVA
Born 1901, St Petersburg, Russian Empire
Died 1993, Philadelphia, United States

YURY FELSEN
Born 1894, St Petersburg, Russian Empire
Died 1943, Auschwitz, Poland

GAITO GAZDANOV
Born 1903, St Petersburg, Russian Empire
Died 1971, Munich, Germany

GALINA KUZNETSOVA
Born 1900, Kiev, Russian Empire
Died 1976, Munich, Germany

These four writers fled their homeland, along with up to two million other White Russians, as a result of the 1917 revolutions and subsequent Civil War. Settling in Paris, Berlin and other cities, they published their work in exile in émigré journals and magazines.

'Kunak' appeared in the collection *Utro* in 1930; 'The Murder of Valkovsky' and 'A Miracle' in the Paris-based journal *Vstrechi* in 1934; and 'Requiem' in the New York-based *Novyi zhurnal* in 1960. With the exception of 'A Miracle', these stories have been taken from the anthology *Russian Émigré Short Stories from Bunin to Yanovsky* (2017).

Four Russian Short Stories

Translated by Bryan Karetnyk

PENGUIN BOOKS

PENGUIN CLASSICS

UK | USA | Canada | Ireland | Australia
India | New Zealand | South Africa

Penguin Books is part of the Penguin Random House group
of companies whose addresses can be found at
global.penguinrandomhouse.com.

This selection first published 2018
003

Set in 12/15 pt Dante MT Std
Typeset by Jouve (UK), Milton Keynes
Printed in Great Britain by Clays Ltd, Elcograf S.p.A.

ISBN: 978-0-241-33976-3

www.greenpenguin.co.uk

MIX
Paper from
responsible sources
FSC® C018179

Penguin Random House is committed to a
sustainable future for our business, our readers
and our planet . This book is made from Forest
Stewardship Council® certified paper.

Contents

Kunak
by Galina Kuznetsova

A little after nine o'clock in the evening, the order was given to set out.

From the station, a string of carts surrounded by people trailed slowly through the suburbs. Almost nobody knew where exactly the embarkation would take place.

Beyond the suburbs, a narrow, stony road led through the darkness, among some bare, thorny bushes. To one side, above the town, a far-off blaze could be seen: somewhere was already burning. The broad white beams of the town's searchlights were fraughtly flitting across the sky. They walked in pained silence, broken only by the cries of the drivers. The twisting road led up into the hills and down again into a hollow. The wheels creaked despondently over the hardened earth. At first they were cold, but the arduous walk gradually warmed them.

No one spoke. In the beginning it seemed to everyone that the sea shouldn't be far off, over the nearest knoll, and everyone stared fixedly into the dark. But the road looped round again and again, knoll gave way to knoll, little stones stung the feet, and the carts rocked helplessly in front of their eyes . . . It was especially difficult for the women in their high winter galoshes and long coats. Yet they carried on more patiently than the men, trying not to lag behind their carts, struggling with the fatigue of many days, with the ardent desire to sit down and rest awhile.

At last, something flickered up ahead. Beyond a dark gate, curiously dominating an empty field, a bonfire was alight, its flame red. Soldiers were warming their hands by it. From the darkness blew a sharp, cold freshness.

'The bay! We're getting close!' cried someone cheerily.

But it proved not to be so. For a long time they walked along the bank, slowly climbing down the hill, when suddenly the carts in front ground to a halt, while those in the rear kept pressing on, and around half an hour passed in agonizing, ever-growing impatience. Finally there was movement, and, before long, far below something big showed black, covered in several rows of tiny lights casting their glimmering gold reflection on to the oily black water.

The column halted at the foot of the hill. Immediately, the regular file of people disintegrated, scattered, and, having snatched their belongings from the carts with astonishing speed, rushed towards the water, where, unusually close to the shore, separated from it only by wide gangplanks, an enormous ship loomed, shining with hundreds of lights. These gangplanks could scarcely be seen for the dense, assortedly rippling crowds that were jostling with one another in a frenzy, shouting, making violent threats.

A small group of women had been pushed back. The tall captain, whom they were watching, swore and shouted in a terrible, hoarse voice that this was the transport of such-and-such a corps, that there were women and children here, that they were 'obligated' to let them through . . . He was met with the same hoarse cries, that everyone here was equal, that it was every man for himself.

Suddenly a coarse, thundering voice, bellowing out from the gangway, overwhelmed all the others:

'Quiet! You damned swine! These are our wives! You're to let them through immediately! What are you standing there goggle-eyed for?'

The enormous double-deck ship was so crowded with people that it seemed utterly impossible to fight one's way forwards. Yet the captain, forever looking about, gave signals to the women, forcing himself to squeeze into a solid wall of burly, bewildered soldiers with knapsacks, kettles and kit bags. The women tried not to lag behind. Meanwhile, in the background, the solid, baying crowd continued flowing in over the shaking, bowing planks, packing the decks, holds and corridors in ever greater numbers . . .

Dawn slowly broke. From the thinning twilight emerged the steel-grey waters of the bay, with wooden barges, rowing boats and skiffs scattered throughout it. In the distance, through the morning mist, the town came into sight, the white colonnade of Grafskaya Pier gleaming white, seeming so tiny from here. The dawn was of icy rose: the steel-grey waters, hazy with a cold, dingy mist.

Packed to the gunwales, the ship settled below the waterline, listing even more towards the shore. By the gangplanks, on which people were still clamouring aboard, stood armed sentries. From the decks one could see the crowd surging below, its arrival from the hill never ceasing, the low expanse of the shoreline increasingly taking on the aspect of some monstrous encampment, with unharnessed carts and unsaddled, wandering horses, their loads abandoned.

Suddenly someone cried out from the upper deck: 'Look, look! There's a horse swimming!'

Everyone turned around. Above the grey misty water, a horse's head could be seen craning. It was swimming apparently without knowing where it was going, borne by the current out towards the middle of the bay. At times it raised its head even higher, and then you could see the water washing over its dark, glossy back. Yet its strength was obviously running out: more and more it would sink, snort and, pinning its ears, stretch out its neck towards the shore, the ship, where it sensed people and from which it clearly expected help. The crowd suddenly fell quiet, forgetting itself, what was going on all around, and began watching it, exchanging hurried, hot observations:

'A Cossack horse . . . It's looking for its master . . .'

'Well, yes, after all, they were told not to take the horses . . .'

'Wait, I know that horse! It's Kunak. It belongs to one of the men in our village, it has the same star on its forehead! It must have swum after him as soon as he had to abandon it . . .'

'It's no secret how a Cossack abandons his horse . . .'

'It will drown!'

'Look, look! A rowing boat, they're paddling towards it. They're going to save it!'

A lifeboat was fast making its way around the stern. It was heading for the middle of the bay. By now strength had utterly deserted the horse, but on seeing the people it sensed, understood, that they were coming to its aid and it made a supreme effort to fight the current and suddenly turned and began swimming towards them quickly. Although it was unclear how they could save this great, heavy horse with their little lifeboat, everyone, with bated breath, forgetting everything else, waited tensely.

'Sternwards, you need to have the stern facing him!' someone in the crowd shouted from the deck.

'Get a rope under him!'

'Look, they've almost made it!'

The horse was already quite near to the lifeboat. Stretching out its fine bay head with a white star on its forehead, it gave out a glad, grateful neigh and with the last of its strength extended its slender, wet neck towards the people. The boat, slowing its course, turned its stern towards the horse. A man in a short Romanov sheepskin coat, who had been sitting at the stern, bent forwards and, quickly drawing his hand from his belt, extended it towards the straining head with its pinned ears . . . Suddenly a short, sharp sound lashed the air. A second and a third followed . . . The people on the shore and those on the boat all gasped in horror and compassion.

The head jerked up sharply in the air, then plunged into the agitated grey water. A minute later it appeared again, but already much farther away from the lifeboat. It was clear that now the current was freely, and with terrible speed, bearing it away. It disappeared again, then reappeared . . . until finally it vanished for ever in the quick-flowing water . . .

The sun was rising. The bright, now vast bay was already aglitter with the sparkle of a mirror. In parts, there was still a fine light-blue mist; the town on the other bank was brightly illuminated, its tightly packed white buildings festively rising up against the mild, blue winter sky. In the east, the peaks of far-away mountains showed mournfully in their many colours, powdered overnight with snow.

A Miracle
by Yury Felsen

I was recuperating after a serious operation. The joy,
such that convalescents experience, was long gone
and had given way to the neurotic boredom of inter-
minable waiting. Those who are often ill know this
impatient reckoning of days and hours, the alarm
if the time of discharge is again postponed, the irrit-
ability brought on by the slightest inconvenience, the
distrust of doctors, who seem to want only to
cash in.

I had my own reasons apropos of this last point,
though they were hardly serious or rational. I found
myself in a new, clean French clinic, in a spacious
and expensive double room, whither friends had
borne me one night in a semi-unconscious state. It
seemed I should inevitably leave the clinic a pauper,
that I was being 'exploited', though the care was
conscientious, even exemplary.

The second bed lay empty, and all I had for com-
pany was an old, no-nonsense physician who visited
me daily and a nurse who for some reason or other
would 'pour out her heart' to me. Tall, stately, no
longer in the first flush of youth, with a faded and
inexpressive ashen face, she would complain at great
length of the intrigues of her *'copines'*, of the quar-
rels between the doctors, of their cavils and their
iniquity. Clinical errors malevolently vivified her, no
matter how sorely the patients paid for it. Another
persistent theme for my entertainment and encour-
agement was her tales of terrible torment and death,
wherein she revealed an uncommon ingenuity.

All this was related to me evenly and with quiet
dispassion, and in the same wise, without raising her
voice, she would unduly extol herself, her experience, her medical successes. Man gradually adapts
himself to any companion fate inflicts on him –
aboard a ship, in a barracks, in prison. And so I grew
used to hearing out attentively the dismal tales of
Sœur Marguerite and lived for the clinic's intrigues,
in a monstrous reflection of my new acquaintance.
I worried that the cleaner was stealing from me, that
the cook didn't know how to prepare food properly,

that the chief physician had confused a stomach ulcer for appendicitis, and my indignant remarks fuelled the sister's loquacity and her inspiration.

I forgot the existence of that former carefree world, which had disappeared for me immemorially long ago and to which God only knew when I would return. Newspapers and books arrived as though from another planet and told of legendary things. Only on occasion would I longingly cast an oblique glance at the empty bed by the wall. I would imagine that my prospective neighbour would once again bind me to that authentic, remote, alluring life to which I was yet denied access. In anticipation I dreamed – evidently having been starved of people – of friendly chats with him, of his relatives and visitors. My acquaintances, in the wake of those first turbulent days, gradually forsook me. Besides, our visiting times coincided with their office hours.

Then, one day, my wish for a neighbour was granted. I was astonished by the exceedingly fussy preparations. In the morning the mattresses were hauled out and shaken in the corridor. The linen was rearranged and changed several times. Two ladies came: a wrinkled, wizened old woman and a slender, elegant, blue-eyed blonde of around thirty, wearing a short (waist-length) fur jacket that imbued her movements with a certain graceful chic. They examined the room and the bed solicitously; the younger lady pulled back the blanket and fluffed the pillows while the older one, patently embarrassed, suddenly turned to me with a strange request to remove to the general ward for two or three days. The sister answered for me, vouching for my composure and forbearance. After the departure of both ladies, she and her much detested *copines* exchanged anxious whispers.

My curiosity had been piqued, but what Sœur Marguerite conveyed to me ere long seemed insufficiently sensational. The nonsense in store was a straightforward operation to remove some abscesses. The patient was a gifted and wealthy engineer; his mother, the owner of some factories; and her companion, his *amie*, who now happened to be his fiancée. It was obvious that the matter was not quite so simple, and my repeated insistence induced the sister unwittingly to give away the secret. The engineer was an inveterate morphinist. It was the consequence of a wound received on the front line and had been going on for more than a decade. He had reached a staggering number: twenty-four injections per day. The syringe accompanied him everywhere, and injections were even done through his clothing, which had resulted in a great deal of suppuration and the need for an operation. Monsieur Morin had been a patient of all the clinics where they battled with a predilection for narcotics, and our staff harboured the vague hope of curing him for ever. Naturally, the ambitious Margarita ascribed the initiative, as well as all conceivable future achievements, to herself.

It was little wonder that this touched me acutely. After my own operation I had experienced unremitting, unbearable pain, and over the course of ten days, every evening before sleep, that same Margarita would inject me with morphine. I cannot recall another so blissful and happy state that could compare with what you begin to feel several minutes after the injection. Somewhere inside there slowly spreads a sweet warmth, your head is enveloped by a clairvoyant drowsiness, pain seems to dissolve, and purposely you try not to fall asleep, so that this inimitable condition might endure without end.

I would awake towards morning (already prepared for the requital) with the anguish of an unhabituated drunkard emerging from inebriation, but tenfold and irremediable. A fierce cold penetrated my body, no matter how warmly I enswathed myself. The pain would return, fortified by bitter comparison – just moments ago I had dropped off so serenely. The day ahead seemed enormous, that vespertine joy almost unattainable, and yet those long diurnal hours were spent in sheer enervate anticipation of the evening. So as to deceive time, to foreshorten it, again and again I would take to counting up to a thousand, call to mind verses from memory, but found it impossible to attain peace. The dear doctor, a punctilious, polite old boy, with a ribbon in his buttonhole, panicked by my formidable passion, worked busily to eradicate it, tormenting both me and the sister.

That is why I sympathized doubly with this man, who was unknown to me and doubtless broken by suffering. I knew the agony of withdrawal, only just having grown accustomed to the morphine's effect, and the agony of escaping it. Of course, in comparison with Morin I had a benign child's ailment, and the more monstrously the ordeal devised for him loomed, the more acutely did he pique my sympathy and curiosity.

He appeared immediately after breakfast, accompanied by both ladies, and I was taken aback by the contradiction between his behaviour and his appearance. A tall, slender Frenchman of almost hackneyed elegance, sparkling chestnut eyes, little moustaches – a picture of smartness and grooming. And at the same time there was a gloomy taciturnity that reached the level of contempt and impudence. He answered his companions monosyllabically and with manifest reluctance; he did not so much as nod to me. I immediately apprehended that no friendship would come of this, that my solitude would be reinforced.

By and by they left him alone, and he took an impossibly long time changing into his patient's gown with his back turned towards me. After around twenty minutes Margarita came in with both ladies, bid them wait, and conducted him to the operating theatre. The women talked quietly between themselves, occasionally asking me whether I was satisfied with the treatment, the care, the food, though they did not inquire as to the nature of my illness. They were interested solely in what was applicable to Monsieur Morin; I, as an individual, did not exist for them. I felt a little insulted, but I overcame myself, deeming the inattention of others natural. By contrast, I admired the fiancée with delight – her strong bewitching hands, their involuntarily graceful gestures, her blonde hair, which tumbled down from under her little peaked cap – and thought, not without envy, that were I in Monsieur Morin's place I would cure myself post-haste of anything for the sake of such a charming lady.

The operation was concluded swiftly, and the patient, so wan and mute, was borne gingerly in on a stretcher. The sister and doctor beamed, averring that everything had gone according to plan. Their delight was imparted to both ladies, and involuntarily I felt aggrieved on their behalf, for Monsieur Morin reacted with icy indifference to their cheerful and ardent congratulations.

He spent two weeks in the clinic, and still never took any notice of me. The ladies were allowed to sit with him far longer than the hospital's rules permitted. He continued to reply to them monosyllabically and discourteously. In their absence he would read some technical manuals or lie motionless in his gown, on top of the blanket, always on his left side, with his face to the wall.

And yet the treatment seemed to progress success-
fully. Margarita, in an agitated whisper, would tell
me how his doses of morphine were being reduced
gradually, how they duped him with injections of
pure water. I could attest in all earnestness to the fact
that he had altered even externally, that his eyes had
become more limpid, his cheeks fuller, the colour of
his face more healthy. Together we railed against
those institutions where he had been previously,
where they took money, promising deliverance from
narcotics, and where they gave nothing in return.
Monsieur Morin would turn away from us in contempt, neither hearing nor seeing our secret
whisperings. The only thing that struck me was his
passivity, his absolute, unquestioning obedience. He
would languidly eat everything the nurses brought
him, meticulously observe the discipline of the hospital, extinguish at the first bidding the electric light
in the evening. Only just before his departure did he
strike up a conversation with me – grimly, drily, without the slightest amiability of tone – opening with a
compliment, which I had neither anticipated nor
merited:

'I should like to thank you before I leave, strange

as it may seem, for not having thrust any unsolicited advice on me. Ever since I developed this unhappy mania, everyone whom the urge strikes has felt it his duty to edify me. It's the same if you aren't set up, if you haven't found a job: thousands of well-wishers take you under their wing – just don't expect a single practical word from any of them.'

I could have objected that my tact and lack of interference had arisen from his hostile inapproach-ability and there was scant need to commend me for this. However, I immediately broke my discretion and could not help offering some 'unsolicited advice'. I told him everything I thought of him:

'You're a lucky man: they tend to you so lovingly. What a charming fiancée you have! Do you truly not want to make her happy?'

'Your reasoning, my friend, is grounded in casual observations, very far from the true nature of things. But allow me to give *you* some advice. Do not believe Margarita; she is a narcissistic halfwit. She has the felicity of being able to alter events to her advantage. Life is easy for such fortunate fantasists.'

I recalled my innumerable conversations with Margarita, and with shame I saw that he was right.

Everything I am writing about her now was essentially prompted by Monsieur Morin; that was the point when I realized, as though it were a humiliation, my foolish credulity and his insight. I do not know why, but he continued his frank confession:

'I am married, I have a remarkable wife who is spirited, intelligent, gifted and beautiful. She left me several years ago in the belief that I would never be done with this vice, that we should never have a home and family. This is an honest *témoignage de pauvreté*. I, too, should have acted thus in her position. The lady who comes here was the governess of my late sister. As you can see, my mother was destined for a great deal of grief. She needs to share with someone the terrible worry she feels for me. She has taken to believing that the sympathy offered by my "fiancée" ' – I could hear the ironic quotation marks in Morin's tone – 'is noble, kind and disinterested. Perhaps she isn't mistaken. In any case, I won't go into details, nor shall I deprive her of these last illusions. My rule is to agree, not to argue, not to object. That way the outside world remains somehow acceptable; I haven't the energy to fight. Sometimes, with no good cause, I hope that everything will clear up, that my wife will forgive me and that an idyllic end to my misadventures is nigh. Obviously, I love her just as I did before. But never mind all that. It's quite improper of me to go on like this.'

He turned away again and spoke with me no more. Only when leaving did he cast a melancholy smile my way. This was ostensibly enough to secure the ingratiating favour of both ladies.

After they left, practically the entirety of the hospital's staff gathered in my room. In came the sisters, the nurses, the thieving cleaner. They summoned the cook and even some of the convalescents. Margarita boasted more than ever. In detail she described her 'method', calling on me to corroborate at every opportunity. I, too, found myself at the centre of attention, though I felt strangely ill at ease. Margarita was congratulated – none too sincerely, but amicably enough – and everyone was left with their respective memories.

She was not able to boast of her achievements for long, however. When they cleaned out the room and the bed, between the mattresses they found two empty phials of morphine and a third, half depleted. I should not have suspected any other demure sister of mercy to have at her disposal such a stock of the choicest curses.

All this almost forgotten history was revived in my memory with extraordinary brilliance when, in the evening paper just the other day, I read that the engineer Charles Morin, an inveterate morphinist, had killed his wife and shot himself without leaving a suicide note. Regrettably, I never did manage to find out who exactly his wife was.

The Murder of Valkovsky
by Nina Berberova

She knew that the man sitting before her was a
scoundrel – it was enough just to look at him, to listen to him, to recall everything she knew about him;
not for a moment did she forget that the man sitting
before her was a scoundrel, and yet still she would
smile long and tenderly at him with those moist lips,
and in her gaze, directed at him, there was such
devotion, rapture, a kind of sweet resolve, so much
so that she came to her senses only after she had
been called for the third time, came to her senses and
understood that she mustn't stare like that, that her
eyes mustn't light up at the sight of this man who
was still a complete stranger, that it was ridiculous.
Above all because he could have been her son, and,
what was more, because he had already danced with
her twice. He had held her so strongly and closely;
she had covered the lapel of his dinner jacket with

powder; she had felt beneath her arm his broad, burning shoulder, and in her hair, at her temple, his breath, which set her mind spinning.

It had been an astonishing revelation that nothing, it turned out, could be divined in this life, nothing could be averted or predicted. Everything that happened happened of its own accord. Even yesterday – as throughout all these long years – she had been calm and wholly satisfied with her serene, almost pure life with her husband, whereas now all that receded into the past – she could remember nothing, see nothing and kept trying to make predictions: if Valkovsky looked at her while sipping from his glass, it would mean that he had noticed her, and if he had, fate could go to blazes. He reaches for the glass and not only does he look at her but he says something to her, very slowly and quietly; he offers her a sip as well, and when she stands up and walks off he follows her with his eyes. Again she thinks avidly that if he gets up and goes after her . . . And so on all evening. As she leaves, he proffers her fur coat. The foyer is dark and crowded; she senses he is about to embrace her, she is struck with terror, her heart pounding so loudly that she can hear nothing but its beat. He slides both his hands down from her shoulders, from under her fur collar, towards her hands, and suddenly grips her fingers violently, all ten at once, and she responds to him just as violently and passionately. She wants to place his hand to her breast, so that he should know what is happening to her heart, she wants to place his hand to her left breast for a long time, for ever . . .

The following morning she awoke with a feeling of shame for the previous evening – she had behaved as though she were drunk, having had nothing to drink; it didn't at all become her. She had grown accustomed to discussing everything with her husband.

'I was beastly last night,' she said apprehensively. 'I don't know what came over me.'

'You were charming as always, quite charming,' replied Gustav Georgievich. 'Valkovsky was trying it on with you, but he's no fool.'

She was now standing in front of the mirror, half dressed, and suddenly she wanted to scream, to sob, to fall flat on the floor.

'Was he?' she asked. 'I didn't notice.'

Gustav Georgievich smiled and went through to

the bathroom, from where, after a couple of minutes, through the half-open door, he said:

'But I did.'

There was only an affectionate teasing in his voice, which immediately set her at ease: she realized that he had no suspicions about what was taking place inside her.

For a whole long hour she remained calm. Then she glanced at the clock, and it occurred to her that Valkovsky might not call at all – not today, not tomorrow, not ever. She could meet him in the street two years hence, and they would have absolutely nothing to say to one another. The prospect made her whole body limp. She lay on the bed – on the wide, warm bed, where she had slept so peacefully in her husband's embrace for fifteen years – and fell into a reverie. It was the heavy, unwanted reverie of a person who has just woken after having slept fitfully throughout the night. The telephone rang. With her eyes still closed, still asleep, staggering and knocking into things, she ran into the dining room. It was her husband, calling to say that he would be late for lunch. She stayed by the telephone, cradling her head in her hands. For the first time in her life she reflected that there was one thing in the world that could not be overcome, that one had to endure: time, the time that would pass between today and that moment when she would be reunited with Valkovsky.

It was a mystery. But for now she didn't have to worry about that. However, she was harbouring a secret: she couldn't countenance the idea that someone might notice the changes in her. Today she would be afraid of appearing absurd, but tomorrow she thought the whole thing would appear absurd – what did it matter to her? For several days she was tormented by the idea that there was something dishonourable about her anxiety, about this anticipation. But this too passed: so what if it was dishonourable! A fortnight went by. No longer did she fear losing everything that she had ever possessed. Even her life? Even her life. And not a moment too soon.

Yet, invisibly to those around her, everything that she was gradually letting go, everything that was slowly but implacably turning tenderness to indifference, and at times even loathing, clung to her, perhaps for the sole reason that they had no inkling that she no longer had any need of them. Hers was the sort of life that every quiet person leads, when there is time to attend a concert, to read a book and in the evenings, by the lamplight, to talk with a companion about the most assorted, anodyne, inessential things, with a companion who for some reason, on account of some long-standing tenderness and intimacy, suddenly at night becomes an occasional lover, ever more bashful with each passing year.

This serene life had on occasion its own similarly benign, peculiarly agreeable plights, coupled with a few little childish joys: for her birthday her husband gave her a large blue lamp, but a week later the lamp suddenly toppled over, and both of them, having been in the room next door, were more astonished than distressed by this, as they picked up the shards and swept away the silvery glass dust. Then a friend who had disappeared in America turned up; later some friends threw a masked ball at their apartment, and her dress, hired from a costume shop, suited her beautifully. Early spring brought the funeral of a girl-friend, who had died while under the knife. And so she went to see the coffin borne out, somehow convinced that she was sure to meet Valkovsky there (all through the masked ball she had tormented herself, too, certain that he would come). And so now, at the funeral, she was once again consumed by the possibility.

Later, despite the vague terror of the days that followed, she still found time to muse about what might have happened, had she not met him on the day of the funeral, how much longer she might have waited, and she realized that she would have waited until he did come, meeting him one way or another, that nothing inside her could be extinguished, that the desire to take his hand and place it to her breast was stronger than anything else, stronger than her very being, that from the very outset she had been ready to pay the price for this.

The coffin was borne almost upright down the narrow staircase, placed into a hearse and covered with a wreath; the mourners, who had been waiting outside on the pavement, got into the vehicles that had been provided, looking just like a wedding congregation with their white roses, and the procession set off through the city. Valkovsky did not sit beside her; he bowed to her from a distance at the doorway. She told herself: 'It's heart-breaking! Marusia – so young, too! And the children . . .' But as she said this, her soul was soaring high above all the words and tears, above all the black, somewhere up in the rose-tinted sky, searching the gleaming windows of the city for Valkovsky's eyes, his smile, invisible to all but her. Even at the cemetery, she felt as though spring had come, although it was only February, and the day before there had been frost.

'How lovely it is,' she said to him, forgetting why they were there, as he walked beside her. 'I think I could come here every day.'

He laughed. They lagged farther and farther behind. Her high-heeled shoes pinched; birds were singing; an empty van trotted past them. Later they stood in a circle and watched as the coffin was lowered on ropes. Taking a trowel, each person in turn threw in a mound of earth; when her turn came, she was in such a state of excitement that she strewed it all down her fur coat.

As they walked back, the crowd continued to thin out, as though the people had connived to leave them alone by and by. At first she had felt the need to latch on to someone (her husband was not there), but she was afraid it would look suspicious. And so they walked together about the city. Where did they go? To drink coffee, of course, to warm themselves up. After all, there had been frost yesterday . . .

She had no desire to talk to him. She was certain they had nothing to talk about, and, what was more, she would never be able to listen to him and answer him. She just wanted to sit beside him, to be near him, to watch him slavishly, waiting for the moment when he would want her. Without hiding behind enigmatic phrases or ambiguous glances, she barters all her self and her life for his desire. No one is leading anyone else. The game is being conducted in the open. His touch is the axis of her existence. Over a cup of coffee, she rests her pale face, still youthful and beautiful, on her hand.

His attack was sudden. What for her had been the first departure in life from that delightful, cunning charade that levelled her with every other woman in the universe, for him was a regular, customary pleasure. He found it slightly disappointing that she didn't put up any resistance, though her sensitivity and responsiveness were enrapturing. There was something within her that took him by surprise, exhausting him. On parting, he noticed that she was in a state of great agitation, that she was expecting something from him. So he told her to come to his apartment again tomorrow.

She had exhausted herself, too. Exhausted, mainly through her bold physical unreserve. She returned home shaken, in a kind of desperate joy, because for the first time in her life she had not seen, did not see, did not want to see herself from without.

'Did you go to the cemetery?'

'Yes,' she said, trying to recall how it had been. But instead, she felt again the approach of avid excitement.

That evening she went to bed early, and Gustav Georgievich came in to bid her goodnight – he still wanted to read awhile. 'Little one,' he said. 'Goodnight, my little one!'

She closed her eyes. The words had sounded so sad, so lonely. But a minute later, she wanted to laugh malignly at him and at the whole world. She clutched the pillow under her cheek and gripped her knees. And her thoughts tripped lightly and gaily back – to Valkovsky.

When the next day she arrived at his apartment, he was just as silent and impassioned as he had been the day before. It was still light in the room, but for some reason a lamp was on, and it seemed to her that it was perhaps not dusk but daybreak. Amid the silence, so effortless for him, there was something that began to alarm her. He smoked in an armchair, while she paced from the mirror to the table, powdering herself, brushing her hair, searching for her gloves and feeling that after a brief hour of happiness something unbearable was commencing: some agonizing mix of fear, doubt and shame.

'I want you to come on Monday,' he said as she passed behind him (it was Thursday). 'Promise me that you'll come.'

She dropped her bag, and her money, a compact and her key scattered on the floor. Slowly she picked it all up.

'What a lot of unnecessary things you carry about,' he said, smiling. He stood up and embraced her.

She pressed herself to him and heard some papers crumple in the side pocket of his jacket. She reached out her arms and embraced him. She felt something hard in his back trouser pocket.

'And you don't?' she replied in alarm.

She was free right through until Monday . . .

She descended the flight of stairs, and this descent from the fourth floor calmed her. All of a sudden she had arrived somewhere – somewhere where she would be alone, where there was still daylight, where it was clear that Valkovsky didn't love her. From those terrible, shaking heights, she had descended to terra firma.

'Why did I do that?' she asked herself. There was a ready reply to this: it was in her body, in her palpitating heart, in her weak, unruly knees, in her eyes that suddenly filled with tears.

'Because I wanted it. Because I needed it.'

Gustav Georgievich was already at home, and now they sat down to dinner. He was, as ever, cheery and equable, but she didn't notice him: to laugh at him was no longer what she wanted. She wanted to be left alone, neither to see nor hear him. That evening they were invited out, and so she went and chatted bravely with a smile. It was two o'clock in the morning when they went to bed and turned out the light; Gustav Georgievich fell silent straight away, and she thought he had fallen asleep. Then she began to think about him – not about Valkovsky, but about Gustav Georgievich – and the tears streamed down her cheeks, on to the pillow, into her hair. So it continued for a while: not a single sob, not a single sniff, she cried in silence. And suddenly Gustav Georgievich's great, dry hand covered her eyes.

'Little one,' he said barely audibly. 'Don't be afraid, come close.'

The darkness made her head spin, she was falling somewhere, speeding into an abyss, unconscious, like one possessed. And only his shoulder could save her from this fall.

'After all, we're together, the two of us, aren't we, little one?' he asked, firmly and chastely holding her to himself. 'The two of us? And we don't need anyone else?'

These simple words, uttered so many times over the course of their life together, now harboured some glad tidings, saving her in her despair. She pressed her lips to his hand. Yes, they were together, and there was no one else in the world. There was no one, nor would there be. He slowly and tenderly, ever more ardently with each passing moment, started to kiss her, taking charge of her, and she reciprocated until they fell silent in exhaustion.

They were together, and they should remain together, and Valkovsky had to be purged from life, otherwise it would be impossible to go on living – he was tertiary. 'I'll do it,' she told herself. 'It has to be done. It's what I want.' Now there was neither temptation nor excitement in her recollection of him. She had waited for an assignation with him, now she would wait for her liberation from him. Otherwise, neither she nor Gustav Georgievich could live.

The only thing she recalled from her most recent rendezvous was that when she embraced him she had felt something like a revolver in his back trouser pocket. The thought of the revolver kept returning to her; there was a tranquillity in this thought, a certainty that here lay the path to absolute freedom from Valkovsky. There was no fear, she wanted his death, just as these two months she had wanted the man himself.

Over these two months she had taught herself to guard her secrets and now she also learned to hide the fact that she had crossed from trepidation and greed to constancy and patient, cold expectation. 'On Monday,' she thought, enduring three long days and gradually realizing that if something unforeseen were to happen on Monday – an earthquake, a revolution – it would not save Valkovsky; she would find him, some day, as she had done before.

'Even her life? Even her life' – insomnia reminded her, poisoned days when she had been prepared so

bounteously to pay for his love. Now she was prepared to pay for his death, and to answer for it, too,
if necessary – that wouldn't stop her: prison had
never stopped anyone who wanted to kill; it stopped
only those who would have to kill to steal a purse.
And when Valkovsky was no more, she would know
that it was just the two of them in the world: Gustav
Georgievich and she.

On the day when it happened, on the Monday, just
after five o'clock, she entered the doorway of the
building where he lived. Her face was luminous,
bright, joyful, just as it had been a week ago when
she had seen off the coffin of her dead friend. She
entered the lift – no one saw her. She rang. But
nobody opened the door. She rang a second time.
Silence. She noticed a key sticking out of the door:
Valkovsky must have run out for cigarettes or pas-
tries . . . She went in. From the vestibule the door to
his room was ajar, and for some reason it was completely dark inside, as if the shutters had not been
opened since yesterday and the curtains had not
been drawn back. She groped for the switch and
turned on the light. Time had stopped: here it was
still Sunday evening, late at night, supper not yet

cleared away, a jacket hung on a chair, cigarette ends in an ashtray, bottles, and Valkovsky himself, lying in bed, very pale, covers drawn up to his chin, a hole in his temple, long cold, long dead.

Someone had taken revenge here yesterday, calmly and premeditatedly, aiming at the sleeping man.

She drew her hand across her face and shuddered. No, the revolver was no longer in his trouser pocket: the pocket had been turned inside out. Again she went over to the bed. By the bed head, on the rug, something sparkled: she picked up a long, thin crystal earring. Silence. Someone had been here before her. They had not finished drinking the bottle – two full glasses stood on the table – but they had managed to eat a chicken, picking at the bones to their hearts' content. Silence. The light had to be switched off. But how young he was! and truly, he might have been her son. Silence in the hallway, silence on the landing. We'll leave the key as it was. Silence below, in the lift. A gentleman and a lady come in from the street. Who could be frightened by that? The earring she placed in her handbag. 'What a lot of unnecessary things you carry about . . .'

And so she is left alone with Gustav Georgievich.

Requiem
by Gaito Gazdanov

It happened in the cruel and wretched period of
the German occupation of Paris. Ever greater terri-
tories were being consumed by war. Hundreds of
thousands were advancing along Russia's frozen
roads; wars were being waged in Africa; bombs were
exploding across Europe. In the evenings Paris was
plunged into an icy darkness; no streetlamps were
lit, and there were no lights in any of the windows.
Only on a rare winter's night did the moon illumin-
ate this frozen, almost spectral city, sprung out of
someone's monstrous imagination and forgotten
in the apocalyptic depths of time. An icy damp
persisted in the tall buildings whose heating had
been cut off long ago. In the evenings, inside apartments whose windows had been blacked out with
curtains, the glass panel on the wireless would
glow, and through the crackle of static a voice

would proclaim: '*Ici Londres. Voici notre bulletin d'information . . .*'

The people were shabbily dressed; few now dared to go out into the streets, and the motor traffic had disappeared long ago. Many went about the city in horse-drawn carriages, and this only served to intensify the tragic surrealism in which the whole country had been living for a number of years.

It was during this time that one day I went to a little café in a suburb of Paris, where I had arranged to meet a casual acquaintance. It was evening, in the bitter winter of forty-two. The café was crowded. By the bar, well-dressed people – scarves, fur collars, pressed suits – were drinking cognac, liqueurs, coffee with rum and eating ham sandwiches, the likes of which I had not seen in a long time. I later discovered the reason for this ham, this cognac and all the rest: the regulars of the café in which I happened to find myself were Russians who traded on the black market. Before the war, in those peaceful, well-fed times, the majority of these people had been unemployed – not because they couldn't find work, but because they did not wish to work, on account of some incomprehensible, stubborn desire not to live as everyone else did: going to the factory, taking a room in some miserable hotel and drawing their wage once every fortnight. These people lived in a state of chronic and, more often than not, unconscious revolt against the European reality surrounding them. Many of them had spent nights in shacks knocked together from wooden planks, looming darkly in dilapidated, abandoned lots on the outskirts of the city. They had known all the dosshouses in Paris, the scant yellow lighting above the iron beds in the enormous dormitories, the dank chill of these unhappy spots and their permanent sour stench. They had known the Salvation Army, the dives and squalid cafés of Place Maubert, where the fag-end men gathered, torpid slumber on benches in the underground metro stations and endless wandering around Paris. Many had travelled farther afield, roaming the French provinces – Lyons, Nice, Marseilles, Toulouse, Lille.

Once the German army had occupied more than half the territory of France, an unusual change took place in the lives of these people. They were given a sudden, wonderful opportunity to get rich – without any especial effort and, essentially, almost without working. The German army and its affiliates would buy wholesale – no haggling – every item that was offered to them: boots and toothbrushes, soap and nails, gold and coal, clothes and axes, leads and machinery, cement and silk – everything. These Russians became intermediaries between the German buyers and the French merchants selling their wares. And so, as in an Arabian fairytale, yesterday's unemployed grew rich.

Now they lived in cosy apartments, which their previous owners had been forced to vacate, leaving behind paintings with obscure subjects, fine rugs and comfortable armchairs. They wore gold watches with gold wristbands, and their fingers were weighed down by rings with genuine precious stones. Behind each of them lay a difficult life – the cities, roads and streets of various countries, huge distances that had been traversed on foot – and here, now, they had arrived at what they had never before been able to dream of.

In the beginning I had come to know one of them – Grigory Timofeyevich, a wiry man past the first flush of youth, with deep-set eyes and a pointed chin. I had met him at a friend's house, a former singer, who in his time had performed in cabarets and cafés. Though back then, when I knew him, all that was already a thing of the past. He had been taken seriously ill with consumption and rarely got out of bed. Every time I visited him, however, lifting his thin hands, he would remove from the wall an enormous guitar that sounded like a piano and in his deep voice, which astonishingly bore no trace of his illness, he would sing all manner of romances and songs – and the richness of his repertoire truly amazed me. Grigory Timofeyevich had known him since childhood; both of them were originally from some village near Oryol. Nobody, except for me, ever called Grigory Timofeyevich by his name and patronymic – he was always Grisha, or Grishka. No one, on the other hand, would ever call the singer by his given name alone – everyone called him Vasily Ivanovich.

'Vasily Ivanovich, I've bought myself a painting,' said Grisha. 'Oh, and I've brought you a roast chicken.'

'Thank you, Grisha,' said Vasily Ivanovich. 'What's the painting you've bought?'

'It's no ordinary painting, Vasily Ivanovich. I paid so much money for it, it doesn't bear thinking about. But the subject is just marvellous.'

'What's it a painting of?'

'It depicts, Vasily Ivanovich, a huge eagle; he's flying somewhere, but on his back, you see, is a very young boy, whom he seems to be carrying away. I may not understand it entirely, but the eagle, I'm telling you, is the finest there is. I've looked at the painting so often – and every time I think the same thing. It's such an incredible painting, there's no denying it.'

'Who's the artist?'

'That, I don't know,' said Grisha. 'Someone very famous. The vendor told me his name, but I've forgotten it. All I remember is that he said Repin couldn't hold a candle to him. He told me the title of the painting too, but, you see, I didn't even register it, so much had it taken my breath away.'

I saw this painting later in Grisha's apartment: it was a copy of Rubens' *The Rape of Ganymede*.

Still, all (or almost all) the clients of that café were buying up paintings back then, just as they would buy gold trinkets and coins. Within these people, who had never owned anything before, some brash, chaotic desire to acquire and possess had suddenly awoken, although it scarcely resembled the Western practice of mechanically amassing money. They would expend ever greater sums of money, paying without thought or necessity, with a sort of peculiar absurdity. I remember one of them, a tall, melancholy man with a black beard; his name was Spiridon Ivanovich. He had been standing in the café, drinking cognac. A glazier had been coming along the street, crying in his plaintive voice:

'*Vitrier! Vitrier!*'

'I can't listen to that shouting,' said Spiridon Ivanovich. 'I just can't, my nerves won't cope. And anyway, he's no reason to shout like that. Who on earth needs him?'

His cry again reached us from the street.

'*Vitrier! Vitrier!*'

Spiridon Ivanovich ran out of the café, went up to the glazier and said to him in Russian:

'For Christ's sake, stop harrowing my soul with all your shouting. Shut up! How much do you want for all this junk?'

Then, suddenly remembering himself, he repeated his question in broken French. The glazier, amazed, hesitantly gave his reply. Spiridon Ivanovich extracted his wallet, paid however much the goods cost, waited for the glazier to leave and returned to the bar

to finish his cognac, which somehow gurgled and bur-
bled loudly in his throat and was accompanied by the
motion of his pointed Adam's apple up and down.

'You slave away all day,' muttered Spiridon
Ivanovich, 'nuisances from dawn, they haven't delivered this, the goods haven't turned up there, and
then someone harrows your soul. The evening's the
only time I get any peace and quiet. I come home,
turn on the heating and lie in bed. I lie there and
think: you've done it, Spiridon Ivanovich, you've
finally made it. Well, chaps, it's time now to get
some rest, not to have a go at glaziers, but to rest.'

'The next world's for resting, Spiridon Ivanovich,'
said Volodya, an athletic man of forty and an expert
in gold. 'I don't suppose there'll be any glaziers there.
What glass have they? Just clouds and angels, nothing else.'

'There won't be any gold either,' said another of
the patrons.

'Of that we cannot be certain,' said Volodya. 'I
once went to Notre-Dame. They had a box there for
donations. I took a closer look and saw that it bore
an inscription: "For the souls in purgatory". Clearly
some funds do get through.'

'That's their Catholic ways,' said Grigory Timofeyevich. 'Naturally, the money goes to the Church, so that they pray for the people they think are in purgatory. But you're right there. It's strange, of course, the inscription.'

For some reason, the day on which Spiridon Ivanovich delivered his monologue had remained curiously fixed in my memory: the hoarse sound of his voice, the motions of the Adam's apple on his long, thin neck, and those words – 'Well, chaps, it's time now to get some rest' – I recalled the expression in his weary, drunken eyes, the winter twilight and the mix of alcoholic smells in the café.

When Grigory Timofeyevich left, Volodya said to me:

'I should never have mentioned the hereafter, I ought to have kept my mouth shut. I worry about Grisha, we all pity him. He's a good fellow, but he's not long for this world. He's been ill for so long.'

Then Volodya began relating to me all his business affairs. His chat, as ever, was overflowing with jargon – percentages, alloys, carats, some or other cut of a stone. It was obvious that he had scarcely been able, in the brief period that had elapsed since the day the Germans marched into Paris, to master all these things. When I once asked him where he had managed to acquire all this knowledge, he told me that he had always been interested in everything to do with gold and jewellery. Before the war, he, like all his friends at the café, had been mostly unemployed and often homeless. But he had spent hours standing in front of jewellers' shop windows on rue de la Paix and reading technical books with the aid of a dictionary, learning the melting points of certain metals and which branches of industry used platinum – and so this formerly shabby, almost destitute man had been able to become an expert in the jewellery business. Before the war, however, his interest in all this had been of a completely abstract nature, and he had never imagined that the day would come when this inaccessible, shop-window gold would suddenly fall to his own hands. According to him, he had met his match only once: a Dutchman with a fair beard and light-blue eyes, a famous safe-cracker with whom Volodya had shared a cell for a few hours in the Central Paris Prison, where he had landed on the charge of vagrancy – that is, for having no money, nor any fixed address.

Looking at Volodya, I would often find myself thinking about how hypothetical so-called social distinction could be: this homeless man ought to have been the owner of a large jeweller's shop on rue du Faubourg Saint-Honoré.

Other patrons of the café, friends of Volodya and Grigory Timofeyevich, lacked such distinct individuality. They all knew how to drink, how to spend vast sums of money; the majority of them had wives or lovers of a very certain type – retouched photos on the covers of women's magazines, blondes in fur coats bought through a connection with some desperate Jew who had already packed off his family to a safe location and now, risking his own life, was selling off everything left in his fur shop. The café's clientele would spend whole days on the telephone, waiting for their next consignment, and in the evenings they played cards, chalking up vast sums of money.

Grigory Timofeyevich said to me:

'Of course, I live well these days. But I see now that I used to dream of all the wrong things. For example, I remember this one night in Lyons, in winter. I had no money, no work, no lodgings. I was sleeping on a building site – at least there was a roof to keep the rain off, if nothing else. It was cold, and I had nothing to cover myself with. I lay there, you know, on some wooden boards, unable to get to sleep – I had no way of getting warm. And so I dreamed. Here, I thought to myself, is an apartment for you, Grigory Timofeyevich, with central bloody heating, and a bed with sheets. And in the evening my wife would serve dinner: sausages, hors d'œuvres, steak. That would be the life.'

His eyes grew thoughtful.

'Though it turns out that all that was wrong. That isn't what matters in life. Or rather, it's not the only thing that matters. What does matter, I don't know – I just know it isn't this. Now I have all those things: the apartment, the dinner, the wife, and even a bathtub – I want for nothing. And yet, that's not quite true. Or so I'm now of the opinion. Say a man gets into difficulties, or finds himself destitute. The idiot will think that's his only problem. But for this poverty, everything would be fine. All right, then. Whisk him off, like in a fairytale, give him clothes, shoes, an apartment and all the rest, and tell him, "Right, then – now live, be merry!" But how do you give him happiness? In a bathtub? See here, I've got a Longines wristwatch

49

that I bought off Volodya. I paid more for it than I would have had to live on for half a year in the old days. I look at the hands on it, and what do they say? It's obvious what they're saying: we're counting down the hours for you, Grigory Timofeyevich. It was five o'clock, but now it's six. That's one hour less to live.'

Now he really did look at his watch.

'Seven o'clock? Another hour gone. But I'm not afraid. There's only one thing I regret: that I've lived for so many years without knowing where human happiness is to be found. Yes, it's all well and good that I've warmed myself, had a bite to eat and drunk my fill. But now what?'

A fortnight somehow passed without my visiting the café. Then, late one evening in February, I went there. Grigory Timofeyevich was nowhere to be seen, and when I asked where he was, I was told that he was ill, laid up in bed. I set off immediately for his apartment, as he lived nearby.

He was lying in bed, emaciated and unshaven, his eyes were bloodshot and sad. At the head of his bed, beneath the light of the chandelier, the wings of Rubens's eagle shimmered with their dark-blue light. I asked him how he felt. 'Not well,' came the reply.

'The quilt feels heavy,' he said. 'It's the last sign. The end is nigh. I'll die – and I still won't know what it was that my life was missing.'

He died during the night, three days after my visit. Volodya told me:

'Grigory Timofeyevich has passed away. He'll be buried tomorrow. Will you come? There'll be a service at his apartment at four o'clock in the afternoon.'

Volodya had never called Grigory Timofeyevich anything other than Grisha or Grishka; until that moment I had not even been sure that he knew his patronymic. I now had the impression that while it was Grisha who had lived, it was someone else who had died – Grigory Timofeyevich. The following day, as I arrived, I witnessed Grigory Timofeyevich's entire apartment overflowing with floral wreaths. Where Volodya had obtained all these flowers, in the February of forty-three, in starving Paris, and how much they had cost, I could scarcely imagine. All the patrons of the café, friends of Grigory Timofeyevich's, were already there, all with that same, uniform, almost indistinguishable face that people have in such circumstances.

'We're waiting for the priest,' whispered Volodya. The priest, an elderly man with a voice hoarse from the cold, arrived a quarter of an hour later. He wore a threadbare cassock, and his countenance was sad and weary. As he entered, he crossed himself, and his lips silently mouthed some phrase or other. In the coffin, decked with flowers, lay the body of Grigory Timofeyevich, in a black suit, his dead face, it seemed, looking towards the sky, where the eagle soared, carrying off Ganymede.

'Where was the deceased from?' asked the priest.

Volodya replied: from such-and-such a district in Oryol Province.

'A neighbour, so to speak,' said the priest. 'I'm from thereabouts myself, not even thirty *versts* away. What a pity, I didn't know I was coming to bury someone from those parts. What was his name?'

'Grigory.'

The priest remained silent for some time. It was clear that this detail – that the deceased was from the same place as he was – had made a particularly deep impression on him. He might have been thinking, 'So this is what we've come to.' Then the priest sighed, crossed himself again and said:

'Were these different times, I'd have served the full requiem for him, like they do in the monasteries. But my voice is weak, and it would be difficult for me to sing it by myself, so may God grant that I make it through the shorter one. Perhaps one of you could help me by joining in, supporting me?'

I glanced at Volodya. The expression on his face was such that I should never have imagined – tragic and solemn.

'Serve it, Father, like you would have done in the monastery,' he said. 'We'll support you, we'll do it properly.'

He turned to his friends, raising both his arms aloft in what seemed like a commanding and familiar gesture – the priest looked on in astonishment – and began the requiem.

Nowhere and at no other time have I ever heard such a choir, either before or after that day. The entire stairwell of the building where Grigory Timofeyevich had lived was soon full of people who had come to listen to the singing. The choir, led by Volodya, sang the responses to the priest's gravelly and mournful voice.

'*Truly, all is vanity, and life is but a shadow and a*

dream. *For in vain doth every man born of this earth disquiet himself, as saith the Scripture. When we have acquired the world, then do we take up our dwelling in the grave, where kings and beggars are the same.'*

And then once again that merciless reminder:

'Such is this life of ours: verily, it is a flower, and smoke, and the morning dew. Come, therefore, and let us look upon the grave. Where is the beauty of the flesh? Where is youth? Where is the brightness of the eye, where the beauty of the complexion? Everything is withered like grass; everything is vanished.'

When I closed my eyes, it began to seem as if the mighty voice of one man were singing, now rising, now falling, and its sonorous swell filled the whole space around me. My gaze came to rest on the coffin, and at that moment the choir sang out:

'I weep, and with tears I lament, when with understanding I think on death and see how in the grave there sleeps the beauty that was once fashioned in His Image, yet is now shapeless, ignoble and bare of all grace.'

Never had I found the requiem so moving as I did on that gloomy winter's day in Paris. Never had I felt with such a convulsive jolt that human genius had perhaps never achieved such terrible perfection in anything as it had in this combination of searing, solemn words and in the swelling body of sound from which they emerged. Never before had I comprehended with such piercing hopelessness the irresistible approach of death for everyone whom I knew and loved, for whom the singing choir offered up that prayer:

'With the Saints give rest . . .'

And I thought that in this terrible hour, which would grimly seek out even me, when everything for which it was worth living would cease to exist, no words and no sounds, apart from those I now heard, would be able to express that finality, beyond which there was no conception of what life was, nor any understanding of what death was. This was what mattered, and nothing else.

'For everything will end and we all shall die: kings and princes, judges and potentates, the rich and the poor, and every kind of mortal man.'

And these very words – searing like hot iron – will sound over the dead.

When the service was over I asked Volodya:

'What just happened? What miracle brought this about, where did you find such a choir?'

'It just happened,' he said. 'One of them used to sing in the opera, another at the musical comedy theatre, another in a bar. Everyone used to sing in choirs, of course. As for the liturgy, we all know it from childhood, just as we shall know it until our last breath.'

The coffin with the body of Grigory Timofeyevich was covered, borne away, placed in a hearse and taken to a cemetery outside the city.

The February dusk fell, plunging Paris into the icy darkness typical of this time of year, and night shrouded everything that had just taken place. Afterwards, it began to seem as if none of this had ever happened, as if it had all been an apparition, eternity's brief intrusion into the historical reality in which we just happened to live, uttering foreign words in a foreign tongue, not knowing where we were headed, having forgotten whence we had come.